Springboard Sports Series
by Alex B. Allen

BASKETBALL TOSS-UP

NO PLACE FOR BASEBALL

FIFTH DOWN

TENNIS MENACE

The Tennis Menace

Alex B. Allen

Illustrated by Timothy Jones

ALBERT WHITMAN & Company, Chicago

Library of Congress Cataloging in Publication Data

Allen, Alex B.
 The tennis menace.

 (Springboard sports series)
 SUMMARY: Andy Wexler decides that this is his
summer to play tennis and enter the local tournament,
but his association with two girls both helps and
hinders his game.
 [1. Tennis—Fiction] I. Jones, Timothy.
II. Title.
PZ7.A4217Te   [Fic]   75-12676
ISBN 0-8075-7773-1

Contents

1   No Court, No Partner,   7

2   One Problem Solved,   17

3   Sheila Takes Over,   24

4   A Lifesaver,   34

5   Backhanded Spoofer,   44

6   Match Point!   54

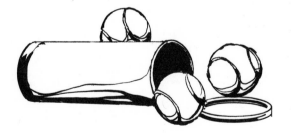

1

No Court, No Partner

This was the summer that Andy Wexler had been waiting for. He was really going to learn to play tennis. Really play, not just goof around, like last summer. He wanted to be as good as his brother Jeff. At least he wanted to be good enough to play in the August tournament.

But he'd hardly had a chance to play. There were only a few tennis courts in town. And they always were being used by older kids, like Jeff and his friends.

"Your serve!" Andy heard his brother shout. Andy was sitting on the grass watching Jeff and his friend Bill play tennis.

"Good return!" Bill yelled. It *was* a good return, Andy thought. He was learning a lot about playing tennis just by watching. But he couldn't learn everything by watching alone. He needed to play a lot, too.

"Hey, Jeff," Andy yelled. "How about a few games with me when you're through?"

"Can't, Andy," his brother shouted back. "These guys have been waiting for the court. Besides, I've got to get to my job."

Andy sighed. How could he get to be a good tennis player if he never played?

He walked over to his bike. He had a basket on the back of it. He kept his tennis racket and balls in the basket. If he ever had a chance to play, he'd be ready. If.

Jeff caught up with him. The boys rode toward home together. "Hey, chum, I really wish I could play with you," said Jeff. "But I don't have much time because of my job at the grocery store. And when I get a chance to play,

I've really got to practice hard. I mean with someone my age who plays my kind of game."

Andy knew that. Jeff's tennis coach at school urged the team members to make their own teams during the summer. He wanted them to keep in shape. So Jeff and his teammates had formed a league. They played summer matches against each other. That meant all the tennis courts were filled most of the time.

But that wasn't Andy's only problem. All of his friends were playing baseball this summer. He didn't have anyone to play with. Even if he could get a court, what good was it? He felt he'd never be ready for the tournament that was coming up.

"I really want to play in that tournament," said Andy.

"Well, you still can," said Jeff. "Anybody can."

"I've got to be better than I am now," said Andy. "And I can't get better unless I practice. I need a partner and I need a court."

"What about Sheila Fox?" asked Jeff.

"What about her?" asked Andy. Sheila was

their next door neighbor.

"She plays tennis."

"I know," said Andy. "I just don't want to play with her."

"I know what you mean," laughed Jeff. "It's no fun being bossed around. But it would be better than not playing at all. Besides, she's not a bad player, and she always seems to get a court."

"I'll think about it," Andy told Jeff. But he'd already decided. Playing tennis was the important thing. He could put up with Sheila. Maybe.

When the boys got home, Jeff hurried off to work. Andy went to Sheila's and rang the doorbell.

A girl Andy's age, but bigger than Andy, with short blond hair, answered the door.

"What do you want?" asked Sheila. "Selling tennis rackets or something?"

"No. I thought maybe you'd like to play some tennis."

Sheila frowned. "With you? Big deal." She glanced at Andy's tennis racket. "I'll play if I can use your racket. Mine's got some loose strings."

This was the way it always was with Sheila.

"Okay," said Andy. It was better than not playing at all, he thought.

"Where can we play?" asked Sheila.

"Elmdale Park. It's crowded now, but we can wait for a court."

"Yeah?" said Sheila. "That's what you think. Come on. I'll show you."

In a few minutes they had ridden their bikes to Elmdale Park. Every court was filled.

"Just a sec," said Sheila. She ran over to one of the courts. Andy watched as she interrupted a game. In a moment the two older girls who had been playing started walking off the court. Sheila beckoned to Andy.

"There. Now we've got a court," she said.

"How did you do that?" asked Andy.

"I told Kim and Mary that Mary's boyfriend was waiting for her at her house. Sometimes you have to lie a little bit."

"Sheila Fox, you're crazy," said Andy.

"Crazy like a fox," answered Sheila. "Come

on. Let's volley for a while." Sheila dropped a ball in front of her, brought her racket around and thunk! the ball crashed into the net.

"That stupid net is too high!" she yelled.

Andy measured it by holding his racket on the ground near the net at the center of the court. He put Sheila's racket sideways on top of it. Three feet. It wasn't too high.

The next volley, the ball bounced into Andy's court and he returned it to Sheila. When she hit the ball, it sailed past Andy out of bounds. "Out!" called Andy.

"It was not!" shouted Sheila.

They volleyed back and forth a few more minutes. Andy began to hit the ball just where he wanted to, getting the feel of things. Sheila wasn't a bad player.

They started playing a game. It was Sheila's serve. She hit her first ball into the net. Andy easily smashed the next one back over the net. Sheila couldn't return it.

"Out!" she called. Andy stared. He knew his ball hadn't gone out of bounds. But if he wanted to play with her, he'd have to play her way. Some tennis partner!

After six games, Andy was winning. He had won four games, and Sheila had won two. Andy looked at his watch—almost time for his paper route.

"I've got to run," he called. "Paper route."

"You're quitting just because I'm getting warmed up," complained Sheila. "I'd have won if we'd kept playing."

They walked to their bikes and started home. "I'm used to clay courts," said Sheila. "That one was cement. It threw my game off. Hey, let's play tomorrow. I want to get better and I need some practice. I'm going to play in the August tournament."

"I'll play tomorrow, but we've got to *wait* our turn for the court," said Andy.

"We'll see," said Sheila.

Andy sighed. He left his tennis racket and balls at home. He rode his bike to the drop-off place for the newspapers. He sat down and started to fold them.

About halfway down the pile Andy found a pink slip of paper. "New customer," Andy said to himself. On the paper was typed: "New Subscription—Theodore Van Epps, 14 Maple Circle." And there was an extra paper in the bundle.

When the papers were folded, Andy stuffed them into the basket on his bike. He had done the paper route so many times he could do it blindfolded. Andy wished he was a great tennis player instead of a great newsboy.

He got on his bike and started delivering papers.

At the end of a short street, Andy came to a little gate with a sign: "T. Van Epps." Through trees and bushes Andy caught a glimpse of a large old house. He pushed open the gate and rode his bike over a winding driveway, up to the front door.

He thought he'd introduce himself to Mr. Van Epps. He could ask him what would be the best time to collect for the paper.

But nobody answered the doorbell. "Maybe he's out back," thought Andy. He walked around the side of the house.

No sign of Theodore Van Epps. No sign

of anyone. But what a huge backyard!

Then Andy saw two empty chairs, a table, and a barbecue grill on a very big patio. "Patio?" Andy asked himself. "That's no patio —it's a tennis court!"

2

One Problem Solved

Andy couldn't believe his eyes. He walked over to the tennis court. "Halloo!" he shouted. But no one was around.

The tennis court was smooth, with no big cracks. At one end of the court was a high backboard. A faded white line ran all the way across it. Around the other three sides of the court was a tall fence—for keeping tennis balls in the court. What tennis balls? Nobody played tennis here. Not with furniture on the tennis court. And no net.

Andy walked around to the front of the house again. He tried the doorbell, but no one answered. Andy shrugged. He propped a newspaper against the door. He got on his bike to finish the route.

Andy couldn't stop thinking about the tennis court. Would Mr. Van Epps let Andy play on it? There's only one way to find out. Ask.

"Even if I could play there," Andy asked himself, "who would I have to play with? Besides Sheila? Well, worry about one thing at a time. Besides, there's a great backboard to practice against. And I could work on my serve. And my backhand. I could get good enough to play in the tournament. Maybe."

When Andy got home, his mother was watering a tray of plants.

"Mom, you know that big house at the end of Maple Circle?" asked Andy. "I guess it's been closed up for a while. But now there's a Mr. Van Epps. He's a new customer on my route. Who is he, do you know?"

Mrs. Wexler smiled and set down the watering can. "If you'd ever *read* those papers you deliver, you'd find out a lot about this town," she said. "Theodore Van Epps is a writer. He lives in California. But he used to live in that house. When he moved west, he left the house just as is, in case he wanted to come back here."

"Well, he's back," said Andy.

"He's going to write articles about Elmdale," said Mrs. Wexler. "He grew up here. He loves it."

Andy poured himself a glass of milk. "I just wondered," he said. "I wanted to ask him a favor. I want to borrow something."

"Borrow something? What?"

"His patio," grinned Andy.

The next morning Andy hurried through his lawn mowing job for Mrs. Larson. While he worked, he practiced what he was going to say to Mr. Van Epps. "Mr. Van Epps, there's something I'd like to ask you. May I use your tennis court as a tennis court?"

Andy decided to ride around for a while before going over to the Van Epps house. Then he changed his mind. "I'm not nervous," he told himself. "I'll go right over there. Right after I ride around the block once more."

Andy found himself at 14 Maple Circle. The gate was open. He parked his bike by a tree. There was a car next to the garage. "He's home," thought Andy. "I hope he's nice. I've never met a writer before. Maybe he's mean."

Andy stepped up to the front door and rang the bell. He waited. No answer. No answer? But a car was here. He rang the bell again.

"Out here!" someone called. "In the back."

Andy walked around the house toward the tennis court. He saw a man with white hair and a neatly trimmed white beard. He was sitting at the table on the tennis court. On the table was a typewriter.

"Hello," said the man. "What can I do for you?" He smiled at Andy.

"Hello. Mr. Van Epps?" Andy asked, putting out his hand. "I'm Andy Wexler, your newsboy."

Mr. Van Epps nodded and shook Andy's hand. "I missed you yesterday. The newspaper was here when I got home. Thank you."

Andy wondered how to start. He *had* to find out whether or not he could play on Mr. Van Epps's tennis court. He glanced around.

"How do you like my patio?" asked Mr. Van Epps.

"Patio?" asked Andy.

"Tennis court. Former tennis court. It's been so long since it's been used, I often think of it as a patio. But today it's my study. Sometimes it's my dining room." Mr. Van Epps glanced up at the sky. "I don't even have to paint the ceiling!"

Mr. Van Epps stretched and smiled. "In California my patio is the size of a postage stamp. This one's as big as a football field."

"Or a tennis court," said Andy.

Mr. Van Epps nodded. "Well, son, I know you didn't come here to talk about patios."

"Oh, but I did!" blurted Andy. "I mean—"

Mr. Van Epps raised his eyebrows and Andy started to tell him about having no court to play on. Mr. Van Epps listened without saying anything. Then he smiled.

"Well, I'll make a little deal with you. This lawn needs a lot of work. And I'd rather work at the typewriter than at the lawn mower. If you give me a hand around here, I'll be happy to let you use the patio—the tennis court. How's that?"

"It's great, that's how it is!" said Andy.

"Then we've got a deal," said Mr. Van Epps. "Come over tomorrow morning. My daughter's coming in from California to visit. She'll notice if it's shaggy around here. You can cut the grass and trim the edges of the patio. There's a lawn mower in the garage, the old-fashioned kind. I'm an old-fashioned kind myself, you see."

Andy grinned. "Tomorrow morning, a date with an old-fashioned lawnmower."

"And ask a friend to join you for tennis," said Mr. Van Epps. "There's a net in the garage."

When Andy rode out of the driveway on his bike, he whistled. At last! A place to play tennis! Now all he needed was a partner. Someone besides Sheila.

3

Sheila Takes Over

That night Andy called all the friends he could think of to ask if they could play tennis. The answer was no—this was their big baseball summer. And Jeff was scheduled to play with his own friends.

It would have to be Sheila.

"Hey, maybe Mr. Van Epps would play with me," thought Andy as he was getting ready for bed. "He must be a tennis player. Otherwise why did he have that court in the first place?"

After breakfast, Andy went out to the garage. He took a pair of grass clippers and put them in his bike basket. His tennis racket and balls were in the basket as always. Then he stuck in a broom, too, and he was ready to go.

Just then Sheila ran over. "Hey, when are we going to play?" she asked. "How about this afternoon?"

"I don't want to push anyone off the courts at the park," said Andy.

"Don't be a scaredy cat," said Sheila. "I got us a court yesterday, didn't I? Well, I'll get us a court today."

"Let's see," said Andy, playing for time. "First I've got a job to do."

Should he ask Sheila to play with him on Mr. Van Epps's court? He didn't want to. Well, he could practice against the backboard. At least the backboard wouldn't lie about things or boss him around.

When he got to the Van Epps house, he parked his bike and walked around to the tennis court. The grass was still too wet to cut.

He decided to trim around the tennis court and sweep it off. By then the grass would be dry enough. By then Mr. Van Epps would be up and around. And Andy would have worked up enough nerve to ask him if he'd play tennis.

Andy hurried. He was eager to practice against the backboard. He was just finishing mowing the grass when Mr. Van Epps walked out the back door and over to Andy.

"Good job," said Mr. Van Epps. "And now my end of the bargain. You can play the rest of the day, if you'd like. Let's get the net from the garage. I'll help you put it up."

It took them only a few minutes. When the net was up, Mr. Van Epps glanced around. "Your partner isn't here yet?"

"No," said Andy. "Do you play tennis, sir?" he asked, crossing his fingers.

"Not for years, son," said Mr. Van Epps. He took out a pipe and put it in his mouth. He sighed. "I don't smoke, either. Not even this old pipe. But it's nice to have around. Just as it's nice to have the old tennis court around, even if I don't use it."

Well, Mr. Van Epps couldn't play tennis. That was that.

"I'm glad my daughter is coming tonight," said Mr. Van Epps. "It's hard for her to get away—she's a doctor. But even doctors need vacations once in a while."

Andy was getting desperate. "Does your daughter play tennis?" he asked.

Mr. Van Epps sucked his pipe. "No, I never could get her onto a court. She never had time—too busy doctoring. So she doesn't know tennis balls from bowling balls. You'll have to find someone else to play tennis."

There was a twinkle in Mr. Van Epps's eye. In both eyes. He sucked on his empty pipe.

"You may use this court. You may use the backboard. But it's going to be up to you to find someone to play with. Maybe there's someone right under your nose. Someone you haven't met yet."

"I'll find someone," promised Andy. "As long as I have a place to play, I've solved half my problem."

"A problem half solved is still a problem

half solved," chuckled Mr. Van Epps, as he started toward the house. He stopped and turned. "Meantime, you can practice against the backboard. That's better than nothing."

"You bet!" said Andy, grinning.

He raced back to his bike to get his racket and balls. And then he ran back to the court. He took the balls out of the can and dropped them, one by one. They bounced well, so they were still good. "I thought they'd have forgotten how," he said to himself.

Andy faced the backboard. He could hardly see the old white line that had been painted across it for the net. He turned to the right and dropped the ball in front of him.

As the ball bounced up Andy brought the tennis racket around. Thunk! The ball bounced off the backboard, about two feet above the pale white line. Andy caught the ball. Got to keep it lower, he thought. He tried again, this time he was just barely above the line. Better.

Andy kept practicing against the backboard. Each time he tried to get himself in position for the ball's return. He was quick on his feet, but there just wasn't enough time to get set for the next shot.

Jeff would tell me to pull my racket back faster, Andy thought.

Then he worked on his backhand for a while. He gripped the tennis racket after turning his hand a little to the right. The first few strokes sent the ball too high above the line.

"Stop scooping the ball," he said under his breath. "Swing evenly and parallel to the ground." He started hitting them more evenly and the ball stayed low.

After a while, Andy felt better about his backhand. But it would never be as good and strong as his forehand. He tried both for a while, hitting a forehand shot, then turning and hitting the next shot with his backhand.

Andy felt good. But it was awfully hard to see the old white line on the backboard. So he went to the baseline of the court and practiced his serve. With only three balls, he had to do more walking than serving.

Besides, his serve wasn't the only thing he

had to work on. He needed a partner to play against. Even Sheila. She was better than no one. Should he ask her?

Andy didn't have to ask Sheila twice. There was no chance for him to change his mind. As soon as she saw the court, Sheila said, "Hey, this is a neat place. And nobody's around."

"I guess Mr. Van Epps has gone somewhere in his car," Andy said. "It is a great court. Just don't bring your friends here. This is private."

"It isn't private anymore," said Sheila. "We're here."

"But that's all," said Andy.

Sheila stuck her tongue out at him. Then she walked over to the backboard. "I can come here and practice by myself if I want to. You'll see."

Andy wished he had never shown her this court. He should have known she'd take it over.

Sheila looked at the faded white line on the backboard. "Hey, this line is pretty dim," she called. "Let's see if there's some white paint in the garage."

Before Andy could stop her, she ran over to the garage. Sure enough, there was a can of paint and a brush in the garage. Andy didn't have time to wonder about that because she said, "Come on, let's paint it."

"We can't do that," Andy objected. "We have to ask Mr. Van Epps."

"We're doing him a favor," said Sheila. She shook the can of paint. "There's plenty here." She started over to the backboard, where she set the can down.

Andy sighed. If anyone was going to paint that line, he was. Miss Know-it-all would only make a mess of it. Just as he was taking the brush out of the can, Sheila grabbed the paint brush, spattering the backboard with white paint. What a mess!

"Oh, do it yourself, clumsy," said Sheila crossly. She handed the paintbrush back to him.

Andy tried to make the best of a bad job. He started to paint the line as neatly as he could.

"It'll take you forever that way," said

Sheila. "You don't have to be so fussy about a silly old line. Just paint it."

"It has to be done right," said Andy. Sheila groaned.

In a few minutes, a car drove into the driveway. Andy wondered what Mr. Van Epps would say about his painting the line on the backboard without asking.

Mr. Van Epps walked out to the tennis court whistling. Andy introduced him to Sheila. "I hope you don't mind, Mr. Van Epps," said Andy, "I'm painting your backboard line."

"It needed it," said Mr. Van Epps.

"I'll say," agreed Sheila. "Hey, I'm going, Andy. I'll be back to play when you're through."

Andy glanced at Mr. Van Epps, who just winked. "You found yourself a partner."

"In a way," said Andy. "She's a pretty good player, but she's a pretty poor sport."

"I see," said Mr. Van Epps. "Well, don't give up hope." He walked into the house, still whistling.

4

A Lifesaver

Andy was up early the next morning. Maybe he could talk Jeff into a game at Mr. Van Epps's. But Jeff said, "I promised I'd fill in at the grocery store for Jack this morning."

"But I've got a special place we could play," said Andy.

"Later, maybe," said Jeff. "I'll give you a chance to beat me."

"I could beat you if you were green and had a long white stripe running across you," said Andy. "My only good opponent these days is a backboard."

"You can't get into any arguments that way," laughed Jeff.

Andy decided to practice against the backboard again. He rode his bike over to Van Epps's. He took out his racket and balls and started practicing.

"Good serve!" he said out loud. "Nice return! Pick up your feet, dumbo, and stay on your toes, the way Jeff does," Andy said as he missed a ball.

"Yeah, pick up your feet," echoed a voice. Andy spun around.

A girl was sitting cross-legged on the grass at the edge of the tennis court. Her heavy black braids fell over her shoulders.

Andy walked toward her. "My partner was too fast for me, that's all."

"It shouldn't be too hard to beat a backboard, Andy Wexler," said the girl, grinning.

"How do you know me?" asked Andy. "I've never seen you before."

"I know you because you're such a great tennis champion. I've seen you on TV."

Andy grinned and sat down beside her on

the grass. She was wearing a bracelet, a name bracelet: Tracy.

He shut his eyes and frowned. "Let me think," he said. "I know I've seen you on TV, too. It's Tracy something, isn't it?"

"You're half right," laughed the girl, pulling at one of her long braids. "I'm Tracy Bennett."

"I've never seen you around here before," said Andy.

"That's because I've never been around here before," said Tracy. "I just got here last night. With my mother."

"You're Mr. Van Epps's *grand*daughter?" he asked. He wondered why Mr. Van Epps hadn't told him about Tracy.

"Very good guess. You win first prize," she said. "I didn't want to come, but Mom made me. I was having fun at home. There's a lot to do in California. And I have lots of friends. Here there isn't anything to do. And I don't know a soul."

"Now you know me," said Andy. "And there's a lot to do." He took a deep breath and crossed his fingers so hard they ached. "Hey, do you play tennis?" he asked.

Tracy shook her head. Her long braids swung. "I never tried it. I can swim, though. I've passed my lifesaving."

Andy sighed. "That's great." He looked up at the tennis court. "What I need is someone to play with. All the guys I know are playing baseball. And my brother and his friends are too busy practicing their own games to bother with me. And I can't play tennis alone."

"You just were," she said.

"I know. But it isn't the same as playing with someone else. Besides, there's a tournament coming up, a big one. And I want to play in it. And I can't unless I get better."

"If you get really good, you could jump back and forth across the net and hit your own balls back to yourself," said Tracy, picking a long blade of grass to chew on.

"I'd be glad to teach you to play," offered Andy. "But—"

"But what?" asked Tracy.

"But nothing. I'll teach you."

"What was the *but* going to be?

"Forget it. What I was going to say was that if you've never played, it would take a long time to show you," explained Andy.

Tracy nodded. "And meantime you'd just be teaching me. You wouldn't be getting in any good games. So your own game wouldn't improve. Right?" she asked, picking another long blade of grass.

"Well, it's all right. I'd like to teach you. After all, if it hadn't been for your grandfather I wouldn't even have a place to practice."

"But I don't know the first thing about tennis," she said. "It would take you all summer. And I'll only be here two weeks, anyway."

"Then let's get started. Here, let me show you how to hold a racket," said Andy, jumping up. "That's a good place to begin."

"Why is there any special way? Why can't I just hold it the way it's comfortable?" she asked.

"It's like this. You say you swim. Well, in swimming there are certain strokes. You learn them because swimming that way is more efficient. It's the same with tennis."

"Already I like swimming better," said Tracy. "Tennis is too hot and it's too hard."

"I'll give you a lesson a day," promised Andy.

"What about a racket?" asked Tracy.

"You can use mine," suggested Andy. "We won't be really playing. I'll just be showing you."

"Just hit it against the backboard for a while so I can see how it goes," she said.

"Okay." Andy jumped up. He practiced hitting balls forehand and backhand. Then he practiced serving. Finally, out of breath, he walked to Tracy.

"Your turn," he called. She jumped up.

It took Andy only five minutes to see that he would never be able to teach Tracy Bennett how to play tennis. Not even if he had all summer. Not even if he spent his whole lifetime at it.

She held the racket like a baseball bat. "It feels good this way," she insisted. "If I can hit the ball, who cares?"

But she *couldn't* hit the ball.

He was right back where he'd started from. Playing alone, or playing with Sheila.

The next day, after Andy had finished mowing the lawn, he rode over to Mr. Van Epps's court and practiced against the backboard. Tracy watched him. At least he had company. And Tracy was much better company than Sheila—Miss Know-it-all.

He was just getting warmed up when he heard Sheila calling, "Hey, why didn't you wait for me?" Andy groaned to himself. He introduced her to Tracy.

"Go ahead and play," said Tracy, "I'll watch, if you don't mind."

It was the same old story. Sheila insisted on using Andy's racket, for one thing. She argued with him about the score, for another.

And she complained about everything. Everything. The sun was in her eyes. He had the best court. They traded courts. Now there was a crack on her side—that's why she'd missed the ball. They traded again. She didn't like the feel of his racket.

But she was getting better. If she'd stop

complaining, stop cheating, stop bossing, and really play, she'd be a pretty good partner. If. If she'd let Andy concentrate on his game. But that was too much to hope for.

Then Andy remembered what Jeff had told him: "Work on your serve. You can win lots of games if your serve is good." So the next day he decided to do just that, to practice without Sheila.

Very early in the morning he rode over to the court and parked his bike. He was walking quietly because he didn't want to disturb anyone. Thunk! He heard a thunk coming from the tennis court. He frowned. Sheila?

He walked around the house. A girl was practicing a strong backhand against the backboard. "Very good backhand," thought Andy. Then he looked again. It wasn't Sheila! It was Tracy.

"Tracy!" he said, louder than he meant to.

She turned around. "Oh, hi, Andy! I just thought I'd get in a little practice before you got here."

She picked up her ball.

"A *little* practice!" shouted Andy. "You're a tennis player! Why didn't you tell me?"

Tracy laughed and swung her racket. "I had to be sure you were pretty good. I didn't want to play with you if you weren't."

Andy grinned. "Okay, that's fair. Now I've got a partner. And a place to play. And ten days before the tournament. Maybe this is my tennis summer after all!"

His face felt all stretched out from smiling.

5

Backhanded Spoofer

"Let's volley for a while before we start," Andy
called. He walked to the other side of the
tennis court and the two started to volley.
"She's good," Andy thought to himself.

Back and forth went the tennis ball as they
got warmed up. They were each learning how
the other played.

Then Tracy served a ball.

"Nice shot!" Andy called as the ball bounced
out of his reach. He returned the next one to
Tracy's forehand and she hit it into the net.

Tracy dropped a ball in front of her, let it bounce, and then brought her tennis racket around. The ball sailed over the net, bouncing again in front of Andy. Andy returned the ball with his forehand. It flew past Tracy.

"Out!" called Tracy. The ball had gone past the baseline of the tennis court. Andy waited again as Tracy hit the ball over the net. This time Andy returned the ball within bounds. Tracy raced over to the ball and hit it back.

"Now let's play a game," said Tracy.

"Fine with me," said Andy.

Andy picked up two balls and took his place on the right side of the center mark. With his left hand he tossed the ball above his head. Then he brought the racket forward, hitting the ball hard. It smashed into the net.

"Fault!" Tracy called. Andy knew that whenever the server didn't get the ball into the other player's service court, it was called a fault.

Again Andy tossed the ball above his head, this time not hitting it as hard with the racket. The ball went over the net and bounced into

Tracy's court. Tracy smashed the ball over the net, to the left of Andy. Racing to the ball, Andy hit with his backhand. The ball hit the top of the net and bounced back into Andy's court.

Andy picked up the ball and walked back to the baseline. This time he had to serve the ball into Tracy's other court.

"Love—15!" called Andy. When the server calls out the score, his score comes first. And *love* means zero.

Andy's next serve hit the net again. "What am I doing wrong?" he asked out loud.

"Try throwing the ball up a little higher when you serve," Tracy called over the net. "And keep your eye on the ball!"

This time Andy got the serve in. Tracy returned it to Andy's right, and Andy hit a hard shot with his forehand.

"Good shot!" Tracy shouted as the ball bounced out of her reach.

"Fifteen—fifteen," said Andy as he got ready to serve again.

They volleyed back and forth for a while.

Andy and Tracy each got two more points and the score was deuce, even. Then Tracy scored a point. One more point and Tracy would be the winner. Both of Andy's serves crashed into the net.

"Game!" shouted Andy. "Boy, I've got to practice my serve."

Now it was Tracy's serve. Her serves were hard and fast, and Andy had a tough time returning them. It wasn't hard for Tracy to win the second game.

"Wow!" Andy exclaimed as they shook hands over the net. "You really play a good game, Tracy."

"Thanks, Andy. But you're pretty good yourself."

"I guess we're evenly matched," Andy said as they sat down on the grass.

"I'm glad I beat you," said Tracy. "Otherwise you'd think that all boys are better at tennis than girls."

"No I wouldn't," grinned Andy. "I'd just think that I, Andy Wexler, am better than you, Tracy Bennett."

"We'll see about that," said Tracy. "My forehand isn't very good. I can never get the ball to go where I want it to."

"Same with my backhand," Andy put in.

"We could help each other, then," said Tracy. "You could hit balls to my forehand, and I'll hit to your backhand."

"Let's try it," said Andy as they jumped up.

For the next fifteen minutes Andy hit balls over the net to Tracy. Each time he made sure to hit the ball so Tracy would be to the left of it. Then she'd have to use her forehand. Andy remembered that in the game Tracy had returned most of his shots with her backhand.

"I see what you mean," Andy called. "If I had seen that your forehand wasn't any good, I could have beaten you. I guess I was too busy to notice."

"I kept you busy on purpose," laughed Tracy. "But it's better for me to learn how to use my forehand than run all over the court trying to hit it backhand."

Tracy then served balls to Andy's backhand. Each time Andy returned one he felt better. "We're improving," Tracy said. "If only I could stay in Elmdale longer, we could both play in the August tournament."

"It's only a couple weeks away," said Andy.

She shook her head and her braids swung, "Mom says I've got to go back with her."

Well, Andy thought to himself, if they played every day, he'd be a better player when the tournament came. Maybe it was lucky in a way that Tracy wasn't going to be around then. He could beat Sheila, but he could never beat Tracy. Or could he? With enough practice he just might beat anyone!

Mr. Van Epps invited Andy to stay for lunch. His daughter had gone into the city for a meeting. His eyes twinkled as he said, "So you found a partner!"

Andy grinned. Mr. Van Epps had known all along that Tracy was coming. He had known that she was a good tennis player.

After lunch, they played again. Andy half expected Sheila to come bouncing in, ready to take over. But she didn't. So Tracy and Andy practiced on their weak spots. They served, returned backhand shots and forehand shots, played close to the net, and tried overhead smashes.

Before Andy knew it, it was time for his paper route.

"I don't know if I've got the strength to deliver all the papers," Andy joked with Tracy. "It's going to take me forever. If I don't make it, you can explain why their fastest newsboy just dropped dead. See you tomorrow—same time, same place."

When he turned into the driveway at home, he found Sheila waiting. "Hey, Andy," she said. "Let me borrow your racket. I played all day with one of the girls and I'm sure I didn't win because of my old racket. Let me have yours while you're delivering your papers."

"Where are you going to play?" Andy asked.

"You know where. Too bad that girl Tracy doesn't play. Or maybe it's good." She held out her hand for the racket and added, "And the balls. Mine aren't bouncy anymore."

Andy started to say, "Tracy's a—" but Sheila

was already out of the yard. "Oh, well," he thought. "Let her find out about Tracy for herself." And he smiled.

Andy went over to Tracy's early the next morning. And Sheila was already there—he might have known it!

"First come, first served!" Sheila called. Andy groaned and sat down to watch.

Sheila was getting better, he saw. She wasn't as good as Tracy, though, and never would be.

"Hey, Andy, let me borrow your racket," Sheila called.

Tracy was tying her braids on top of her head. "You can play the winner, Andy," she explained.

Andy nodded. At least he knew Tracy would win and he wouldn't have to play against Sheila. But the game took a long time. Tennis was no game for three people.

During the next days, Andy always found himself waiting. Waiting for a court, waiting for a partner. And it was Sheila's fault.

No matter how early he arrived, Sheila was

there. She took over the court, and she took over Tracy.

"I can't hurt her feelings," Tracy said when Andy complained. "I can't be rude, and she's a pretty good player. But I'll try to play with you as much as I can."

Even when it was Andy's turn to play with Tracy, Sheila would sit on the grass watching. Watching and criticizing. "Oh, Andy, that was a dumb thing to do." Or, "Andy, your timing is all off."

Five days. Four. Three. Two. One. And Tracy was leaving the next day. "I've got to do my paper route," said Andy.

"And I've got to pack," said Tracy. "We're leaving first thing in the morning."

"I'll stay here and practice my serve against the backboard," said Sheila. "The tournament's day after tomorrow. Leave me your racket, will you, Andy?"

Tracy winked at Andy. He sighed. He wished he'd never met Sheila. He wished she'd move away. He wished she'd drop dead. No such luck.

6

Match Point!

It was raining the next day. Just as well, thought Andy. Tracy was gone. And he couldn't stand playing with Sheila. Not today, anyway.

Saturday came: the day of the tournament! Andy was too tense to eat any breakfast.

When the Wexlers got to the Elmdale Park courts, everyone in Elmdale seemed to be there for the tournament. Not just from Elmdale, either. From all the neighboring towns. Andy glanced around. There were plenty of kids his age. He could have had lots of tennis partners if he'd just known them!

Jeff and Andy walked over to the registration desk. "No turning back now," thought Andy.

Sheila elbowed her way ahead of the boys, swinging a new tennis racket.

At the registration desk officials explained that the player winning nine games would win the match and go on to the semi-finals. Because there were only four courts, there wasn't much time to play the usual tournament rules.

After registration, the contestants sat on a bench at the other side of the courts. People stood around watching them. There were several announcements.

"On court one," shouted an official, "Jeff Wexler and Randy Kincaid!"

Jeff grabbed his racket and jumped up.

Andy watched his brother greet his opponent. Three other sets of highschool boys and girls got ready to play on the other courts.

The games started. Jeff discovered that his

opponent had a weak backhand, and he made the most of it. He hit almost every shot to the player's backhand. Jeff won nine games to Randy Kincaid's five. The match was over and Jeff was the winner.

"Great game!" said Andy as Jeff came back to the bench. "Now what happens?"

"Since there are so few courts, the semifinals and final matches for older kids are scheduled tomorrow," said Jeff.

"Lucky you," said Andy. "Another day to practice."

Later, Andy's group started their matches. Andy swallowed. "Go get 'em, sport!" said Jeff.

Andy walked onto court three and shook hands with his opponent, Rusty Reed—a small wiry boy with red hair.

The first game started. It was Rusty Reed's serve. Andy couldn't keep his eye on the ball, and he lost the first game. "Get moving," he said to himself. He could almost hear Tracy saying, "You can do it, Andy."

From then on Andy took control of the

game. His backhand came to life and he returned difficult shots.

Rusty had a weak serve and Andy made the best of it. He made Rusty run all over the court to return shots. Before long Rusty was tired. He just couldn't keep up with Andy. Soon most of Rusty's shots went into the net.

"Match point!" called the announcer.

Andy's serve bounced out of Rusty's reach.

Game! Match! Andy was the winner. Now he was a semi-finalist. He ran over to the net to shake hands with Rusty.

When Andy went back to the bench, Jeff couldn't stop talking about the match. "Wow! I can't believe it! You were great! What happened?"

"Save it for the semi-finals," laughed Andy. "Then I'll need all the help I can get." Andy watched the other players finish their games. When the matches were over, he would play one of the winners.

Two players, a boy and a girl, were tied on court one. Andy watched them closely, hoping to pick up a few pointers just in case he had to play one of them later in the day.

"Match point!" the announcer called.

Andy watched the girl. She needed one more point to win the match. When the ball was served, she returned it with a hard backhand shot. "Great backhand," thought Andy. Then he sat up on the bench. Something funny about that backhand—he'd seen it before. He gulped. Tracy!

"Match!" called the announcer. "The winner is Tracy Bennett!"

Andy jumped up. He ran onto the court. "Tracy! What are you . . . how did you . . . where's your hair?"

"I cut it off," said Tracy. "Hair today, gone tomorrow. Let's sit down. I've got to rest if I'm going to beat you."

"We'll see about that," said Andy. "You knew all along you were going to play in the tournament."

"Nope," answered Tracy. "Honest. I didn't know until the last minute. Finally I talked Mom into letting me stay. She had to go back to her practice, but I'm going to fly out with grandfather later this summer. Then the officials almost didn't let me in the tournament because I hadn't registered on Monday."

Sheila ran over to Andy and Tracy. "I could have won my match if the sun hadn't been in my eyes on that one game. And my new racket's too light. It wasn't fair." Then Sheila ran off.

Andy winked at Tracy. "If all my tennis partners were like that, I'd give up tennis."

"Attention!" called the announcer. "Now for the intermediate semi-finals! Tracy Bennett against Andy Wexler on court one!"

"Oh, no! I really *do* have to beat you," Tracy laughed and looked at Andy. "Shall we show these people how to play tennis?" They ran onto the court. They volleyed for serve and Tracy won.

Tracy served. Andy smashed the ball into the net. She served again. Andy hit it out of bounds. "Got to concentrate," he thought. "Pretend this is just a regular practice session."

But he couldn't concentrate. His forehand was off and his timing was bad. Tracy won the first game. They passed each other as they changed sides. Tracy said, "You're *letting* me win, aren't you?"

Andy grinned. "Not a chance."

But when Andy served, his ball crashed into the net both times. "If I can't win when I'm serving, I can't win at all," he thought. Andy managed to get a few shots in, but he lost the second game anyway.

Tracy played well. Her serves were in, her backhand was great, and most of all, she was relaxed and cool. She won the third game.

And Andy still couldn't get going. Tracy won the fourth game. As they were changing courts, Tracy grinned at him.

"I've been hitting to her backhand!" Andy thought suddenly. "And I *know* her backhand is a good stroke."

That made a difference. Andy returned as many shots as he could to Tracy's forehand. And he won two games. Then it was four games to two.

The two tennis players battled back and forth. Andy concentrated more. It became a close match.

Seven games to six, and Tracy was ahead. The first to win nine games would be the winner. It was Andy's serve.

His service was still off. He kept hitting into the net. He needed to throw the ball a lot higher. And keep his eye on it. Just the way Tracy had told him.

He started throwing the ball higher. And Andy won the game! The match was tied, seven to seven.

Now Andy felt he could control the rest of the match, but Tracy felt the same way. She was playing as hard as ever, too.

Andy won the next game (his serve)—but Tracy won when she served. So the score was eight to eight.

"Match game!" called the announcer. The next game would decide the winner. It was Andy's serve.

Andy threw the ball high over his head, brought the racket forward and smashed the ball into Tracy's court. She returned it to Andy's backhand. He hit the ball into the net.

Andy's next serve was too hard and fast for Tracy to return. The tennis players each won two more points. Then Tracy neatly placed a shot out of Andy's reach.

"Match point!" called the announcer. One more point for Tracy, and she'd win the match. Andy concentrated as hard as he could. He served the ball so hard that Tracy hit it into the net.

"Deuce!" called the announcer. The game was tied.

Andy's next serve was a beauty. Tracy couldn't hit it. Again the announcer called match point.

Andy tossed the ball over his head and hit it into Tracy's court, but she returned it with a strong shot to Andy's forehand. Andy took position, brought the racket forward, and aimed his shot for Tracy's forehand. The ball dropped in front of her, and she brought her racket around. But the ball hit the top of the net and dropped back into her court. Match!

"The winner!" called the announcer, "is Andy Wexler!"

Andy ran to shake Tracy's hand.

"Great game, champ!" grinned Tracy, "You're a real pro."

"Thanks," smiled Andy. "But I won because of your great coaching. And because I knew about your backhand."

Mr. Van Epps walked over to them. He shook Andy's hand. "Congratulations, Andy. It looks to me as if you've solved your problem. You've got yourself a court and you've got yourself a partner. And a chance at the finals tomorrow."

Sheila called from the other end of the benches. "Hey, Andy! Let's play tomorrow after the tournament!"

Andy glanced at Mr. Van Epps and winked. "Like you say, Mr. Van Epps, a problem half solved is still a problem half solved!"